The Bond

William Fritz

 pencil

ISBN 978-93-5667-540-7

Published in India 2023 by Pencil

A brand of
One Point Six Technologies Pvt. Ltd.
123, Building J2, Shram Seva Premises,
Wadala Truck Terminal, Wadala (E)
Mumbai 400037, Maharashtra, INDIA
E connect@thepencilapp.com
W www.thepencilapp.com

Author biography

William Fritz is a young writer who loves to inspire and shock readers. He is known known for his unique writing style that blends engaging and imemrsive storytelling. His writing explores a variety of themes, from the depths of the human psyche to the darkest corners of the human condition, all while taking readers on epic adventures across fantastical landscapes. Born in Springfield, Missouri, William Fritz has always had a passion for storytelling and using words to capture the essence of the human experience. He draws inspiration from a wide range of sources, including classic literature and contemporary pop culture. In addition to his writing, William Fritz is also a passionate advocate for creativity and innovation. He enjoys mentoring aspiring writers and artists and is committed to helping others unlock their own creative potential.

CONTENTS

Chapter 1

It was mid-october and the crisp automator had settled into the small town of Fenton Missouri the trees in the area were on fire with brilliant Reds and oranges casting a warm comforting glow over the houses and streets below as the sun began to dip below the Horizon it bathed the homes in a golden light making them look as if they were touched by magic the family lived in a two-story red brick house with white shutters although it was not a grand or opulent home it was filled with love and warmth and was a source of comfort for the family the house was surrounded by a well-manicured lawn and beautiful flower beds which were carefully tended to by the wife as the Sun finally disappeared behind the trees the family sat down for dinner at their well-worn dining table they were a happy family and their love for each other was strong however as the night grew longer and the stars came out a sense of unease began to settle in something was not quite right in the town of Fenton and the family couldn't shake the feeling that they were being watched little did they know their lives were about to change forever they were the perfect family at least that's what it seemed like on the surface the husband and wife were deeply in love having met in college and fallen for each other's infectious laughter and kind hearts they had a son who was the light of their lives a precocious 14 year old who was a talented athlete and an Avid Reader they lived in a modest home in the heart of Missouri surrounded by Rolling Hills and sprawling forests that offered an endless playground for their Adventures the husband worked a nine to five job as an accountant a position that he took simply because it provided a steady income for his family he often found himself counting down the minutes until the end of the day longing for the weekends and holidays when he could spend time with his loved ones he felt trapped in his job a prison of sorts and he resented the long hours and the monotony of the work sometimes he would escape to the bathroom at work and cry silently feeling like a failure for not being able to provide more for his family the wife on the other hand was a talented jewelry maker and a stay-at-home mom she poured her love and creativity into her craft and her pieces were sought after by customers both locally and online despite her success she felt lonely and unfulfilled the town they lived in was unfriendly and the other parents at the school were rude and dismissive she had no friends to confide in and she often found solace in a bottle of wine in the evenings her husband was the only person who knew of her struggles and she felt like a burden to him their son though bright and curious sometimes felt like he was caught in the middle of his parents difficulties he was a good kid always eager to learn and try new things but he also felt the tension between his parents he couldn't help but wonder if they would eventually get divorced and he felt sad and alone with these thoughts he was their shining star but he didn't want to be a burden on their relationship despite their struggles the family remained tight-knit and loving they were each other's Rock and they were determined to overcome their difficulties together they would often go on hikes in the forest or have movie Nights At Home and these moments were their escape from the stress and worries of daily life they were happy or so they thought but as they would soon find out their greatest challenge was yet to come John was a man of many responsibilities he had a family to take care of a mortgage to pay and bills to cover he worked a job that he despised but he did it anyway because he loved his wife and son more than anything in the world John was the sole Breadwinner in the family and he took his role as a provider very seriously John's job was dull and monotonous but he didn't complain he was grateful to have a steady income that allowed his wife Sarah to focus on her jewelry making business Sarah was an amazing artist and her business was growing but it wasn't yet enough to support the family on its own John hated that he had to work a job he didn't enjoy but he did it because he knew it was necessary the weight of his responsibilities was overwhelming and he felt like he was trapped in a never-ending cycle of work and bills he longed for a change but he didn't know how to escape the normalcy of his life despite his struggles John never let his family see him cry or feel his burden he was determined to keep his chin up and be the strong and dependable husband and father that his family needed John's love for his family was the one thing that kept him going but the constant stress was taking a toll on him he didn't know how much longer he could keep up the facade of being the strong provider but he knew he had to keep trying the thought of his family's happiness was the only thing that got him through each day but he couldn't help but feel like a failure sometimes despite his struggles Jon Was A Good Man Who Loved his family deeply his burden was a heavy one but he carried it with Grace and dignity he knew that one day everything would be all right and that he would finally be able to escape the normalcy of his life until then he would continue to Bear the burden of responsibility and do what was necessary to take care of his family Sarah was a beautiful and talented woman she was a stay-at-home mom and a jewelry maker she was an amazing cook and her jewelry was popular in the Online Marketplace but despite her talents and achievements she felt alone and isolated the small town the family lived in was a rough Place filled with unfriendly people and a general sense of negativity the other parents in town were rude and unapproachable leaving Sarah feeling isolated and lonely she often found solace in her jewelry making and cooking but it was not enough to fill the void in her heart Sarah had a secret she kept hidden from her husband and son a secret that ate away at her from the inside she had developed an alcohol problem and found herself reaching for the battle more and more frequently she knew it was a problem but she didn't know how to stop she was scared that if she told her husband he would leave her so she hid it from him trying to keep up the appearance of a happy loving wife and mother despite her struggles Sarah was still a loving wife and mother and she loved her family more than anything in the world she was determined to keep up the facade of a happy family but the burden of her secret was weighing down on her making her feel trapped and alone Alex was a curious and adventurous 14 year old boy he loved Sports video games science and learning about new things he was always eager to explore the world around him and seek out new experiences he was a good kid always polite and respectful and his parents John Sarah were proud of him however Alex had a weight on his shoulders that most children his age did not have to bear despite his parents best efforts to maintain a happy and stable home Alex was aware of the underlying tension between them he could sense that something was not quite right and he feared that his parents might get divorced he didn't know what he would do if that happened he felt alone and isolated with no one to talk to about his fears at times Alex would catch his father crying alone in the bathroom and he knew that it was because his job was causing him a lot of stress he also noticed that his mother Sarah was drinking more than usual and he could tell that she was struggling with something he wanted to help them both but he didn't know how despite all of this Alex remained optimistic and hopeful he believed that things would get better and he focused on his passions and interests to distract himself from the chaos at home he was determined to make the best of his situation and to be the best version of himself that he could be.

Chapter 2

The morning sunshine bright on the new day as the family of John Sarah and Alex excitedly got ready for one of John's work events John had received an invitation to his company's annual bowling tournament where the grand prize was a paid time off to be used for a much needed Family Vacation it was a special day as John had been working hard to get a break from the stress of his job and to spend some quality time with his wife Sarah and Son Alex as they all got dressed John couldn't help but feel a sense of nervousness he had never been a great bowler but he was hoping that luck would be on his side today Sarah on the other hand was wearing her favorite red dress looking stunning and ready to support her husband Alex was equally eager wearing his lucky t-shirt and ready to cheer on his dad the drive to the work event was filled with anticipation and excitement when they arrived John was greeted by his colleagues and boss the tournament began and there was a festive atmosphere as everyone was having fun cheering each other on and having a great time John's boss Mr Nelson was a well-respected man in the company but he had a reputation for flirting with the wives of his employees and Sarah was not immune to his advances throughout the night Mr Nelson would approach Sarah and make small talk complimenting her on her dress and asking her about her life Sarah didn't think much of it and just thought that he was being friendly however every time John wasn't looking Mr Nelson would take the opportunity to hit on Sarah he would whisper things in her ear touch her arm and make suggestive comments Sarah felt uncomfortable but she didn't know how to react she didn't want to cause a scene at the event especially since John was having such a great time John on the other hand loved his boss and didn't have a clue about the inappropriate behavior towards his wife he was so caught up in the moment and the excitement of winning the award that he didn't pick up on the tension between his boss and Sarah as the night went on Sarah couldn't take it anymore she excused herself from the event and went to the bathroom to compose herself she couldn't believe that someone she respected and worked for would treat her this way she was feeling violated and didn't know what to do Sarah finally returned to the event and the rest of the night went by without any further incidents however the encounter with Mr Nelson left a bad taste in Sarah's mouth and she couldn't shake the feeling of being disrespected meanwhile it was the final round and John was up he took a deep breath and picked up the bowling ball he aimed and with a powerful swing he let the ball go it was a perfect strike and everyone erupted in Applause John had won the tournament and the grand prize was now theirs the family celebrated their win hugging each other and cheering they were relieved that they could finally go on a well-deserved vacation John was proud of himself for overcoming his fear of failure and Sarah was proud of him too Alex was jumping up and down with excitement eagerly waiting for the forest hike that awaited them the family left the work event feeling happy and grateful they were ready for their new adventure and the vacation that was made possible by John's win at the bowling tournament the night before the family's trip to their cabin in the woods Sarah and John sat on the couch together lost in thought John was the first to break the silence you know Sarah this vacation couldn't have come at a better time Sarah looked at her husband and smiled I know John I feel like we all just need some time away from everything to just be a family as they continue to talk they both opened up to each other about their struggles and how they felt like they were drowning under the weight of their responsibilities John talked about the stress of work and how he was starting to feel like his job was taking over his life Sarah confided in John about the difficulties she faced as a stay-at-home mom how she felt like she was losing herself and that she just needed some time to reconnect with who she was they both agreed that this vacation was exactly what they needed to bring them back together as a family they hugged each other tightly grateful for each other and for this opportunity to escape their daily lives meanwhile Alex was in his room packing his bags for the trip he was so excited to spend some time in nature with his parents he remembered all the fun times they used to have on family trips and how he felt like they had fallen apart in recent years Alex felt a sense of hope for the future as he packed his bags and went to bed dreaming of the adventures that lay ahead for the family the next morning the family woke up early ready to start their Journey they hugged each other and hand in hand made their way to the car they were filled with excitement and anticipation for the journey ahead they all knew that this trip was going to be a turning point in their lives a chance for them to heal grow and come back together as a family and with that they set off ready to make new memories and create a brighter future for themselves the family of John Sarah and Alex are now on their long car ride to the forest where they would be going on a well-deserved vacation hike near a cabin that they owned excited for their Adventure they packed their bags and hit the road eager to leave their daily worries behind as they drove down the highway they came across a herd of deer grazing by the side of the road Alex who was fascinated by Nature was amazed at the site and pointed it out to his parents but their excitement was short-lived when moments later they hid a deer that had wandered onto the road the impact was violent and the car was severely damaged the family was shaken and Alex was crying in the back seat unable to comprehend what had just happened the dear lay lifeless on the side of the road its blood seeping into the gravel John tried to call for a toe but his phone had no signal after a few hours a tow truck finally arrived driven by a smelly cigarette smoking man the man was rude and indifferent to the family's distress when Alex tried to talk to him the man blew smoke into the boy's face leaving Alex coughing and upset John who was already upset by the deer wreck didn't say a word the family was forced to spend the night at a hotel while the car was being repaired it was a creepy old hotel and the family had trouble sleeping in the middle of the night they encountered a creepy old man in the hotel hallway who warned them about the Hidden Forest they were heading to the old man's words were ominous and he told them not to go the lights were flickering on and off in the hallway adding to the Eerie atmosphere despite the old man's warning the family pressed on and continued their

Journey the next day they were determined to reach their cabin in the woods and start their well-deserved vacation hike the road ahead was long but they were confident that their love for each other would carry them through any challenge that lay ahead the next morning the family rented a car from a nearby car store John Sarah and Alex could finally pack up their belongings and leave the hotel room after a long and tiring night all of them were looking forward to their much needed vacation the drive continued with John behind the wheel trying to keep his eyes open Sarah sat quietly in the passenger seat her thoughts consumed by the events of the day Alex was feeling exhausted as well and he leaned against the window his eyes closed as the family continued their Journey on the road Alex later woke up to notice a herd of deer up ahead he quickly alerted his parents who were also taken aback by the sudden appearance of the wild animals the deer were peacefully grazing on the grassy Fields completely unaware of the presence of the Family's car at first the sight of the deers was calming and almost surreal the sun was setting casting a warm glow on the animals making them look almost angelic but as the car approached the herd Alex's heart started to race he couldn't help but think about the danger the deer could pose if they suddenly ran out in front of the car again dad what do we do Alex asked his voice trembling his dad John took a deep breath and calmly replied just stay calm Alex I'll try to drive around them okay John slowly drove the car around the herd trying to keep a safe distance from the animals the family held their breaths praying that the deers wouldn't startle and cause any accidents eventually they made it through the herd and continued down the road but the sight of the second herd of deers left Alex feeling uneasy he couldn't shake the feeling of and kept glancing out the window worried that they might encounter another herd of deers Sarah and John noticed his unease and tried to reassure him that everything was okay they continued the journey with their car humming along the highway passing by Rolling Hills and towering trees Alex dozed off again and when he woke up this time he realized that they were almost at the turn off for the cabin he rubbed his eyes and peered out the window excitement filling him at the thought of finally reaching their destination John glanced at Alex in the rearview mirror a small smile playing at the corners of his mouth almost there he said just a little bit further Sarah nodded a look of relief spreading across her face I can't wait to finally get there and just relax she said the three of them continued on the road they were all tired but they were also filled with a sense of anticipation for what was to come they were eager to reach the cabin to start their vacation and to leave behind the stresses of their daily lives in the end they drove for another hour until they finally reached the turn off for the cabin the sign read almost there and Alex smiled to himself feeling grateful for this opportunity to escape from the normalcy of his life and spend time with his family in the beautiful wilderness the families car finally approaches the turn off to their vacation cabin the road ahead leads into a dense forest the trees towering high above Alex who had been listening to music notices a sign ahead that reads almost there as they drive deeper into the forest Alex's thoughts wander to the two herds of deer they had seen so far on the trip he thinks it's strange that they look so similar but quickly shakes the thought off as the family continues on Alex takes in the beauty of the forest the sounds of nature surround them and the occasional flicker of sunlight piercing through the trees he feels a sense of Peace wash over him as they make their way through the forest despite the unsettling events of the past few days just as he thinks they might have arrived at the cabin Alex spots another herd of deer ahead he watches as they Dart across the road and disappear into the underbrush he can't help but wonder if they'll ever get to the cabin but he decides to push those thoughts aside and enjoy the peace and serenity of the forest as the family drove through the dense forests of their vacation destination the sky grew darker and darker the once Blue Sky was now a deep shade of blue signaling that a storm was approaching Alex who was lost in his own world listening to music didn't seem to notice the change in weather meanwhile John and Sarah were having yet another argument this time about the bills they were so engrossed in their argument that they failed to realize that the sky was becoming more ominous by the minute suddenly a massive bolt of lightning struck a nearby electric pole knocking out the power to the only light that was guiding their path the Family's car was plunged into complete darkness and they could barely see the road ahead the sound of the rain hitting the roof of the car was now the only source of noise John who was driving had to slow down and navigate the car through the rain and the Darkness

Chapter 3

As they continued to drive the darkness seemed to be closing in on them the road ahead was shrouded in an eerie blue glow and the trees on either side of the road looked like ghostly figures in the Darkness the once peaceful forest was now an ominous and frightening place Alex who had finally noticed the change in weather was now wide-eyed and alert he wondered why his parents had not stopped the car to wait out the storm John who had been driving in silence for the past few minutes finally spoke up we're almost there he said trying to calm his family we're only 15 minutes away from the cabin but Sarah was not so easily convinced she was starting to regret coming on this vacation in the first place and the Eerie Darkness only made her feel more apprehensive despite the frightening conditions the family pressed on determined to reach their destination the rain was coming down harder now and the wind was howling through the trees but they were determined to reach the cabin and so with a sense of both fear and determination the family continued their Journey Through The Dark and Stormy Night eager to reach their destination and escape the Eerie Darkness the family had been driving for hours and it seemed like the storm was never going to end the rain pounded against the windows of the car and the wind held making it difficult for them to see the road ahead John

Sarah and Alex were all tired and exhausted from the drive but they were still excited to finally reach their destination however as they continued to drive they began to realize that they were not as close to the cabin as they thought they would be the sign that said almost there had been almost in 30 minutes ago and they still hadn't arrived the family started to wonder if they had taken the wrong turn and the argument that had been brewing between John and Sarah started to escalate as they drove deeper into the forest they suddenly saw another sign that red almost there the sign was old dirty and barely visible it was surrounded by a herd of deers who were watching the car with unblinking eyes the family was starting to get worried and John tried to calm Sarah down but she was insistent that they had taken the wrong turn as they drove the scenery around them started to change the trees became taller and denser blocking out what little light was left from the stormy sky the road was narrower and bumpier and the family was starting to feel like they were lost however they continued to drive determined to reach the cabin the family drove into the night the only light coming from the headlights of the car the rain continued to fall and the wind howled making it feel like they were the only people in the world they were all exhausted but they couldn't stop thinking about finally reaching their destination and having a much needed vacation as Alex dozed off he couldn't help but wonder why they still hadn't arrived at the cabin the sign that said almost there had been almost an hour ago and they still hadn't arrived he was starting to feel worried but he was too tired to say anything suddenly he was jolted awake by John's voice wake up Alex we're almost there John said pointing out the window to a sign that red almost there Alex rubbed his eyes and looked out the window trying to shake the drowsiness he looked at the sign and then at his dad confusion etched on his face why did you wake me up for this Dad we've seen this sign over and over Alex said his voice groggy from the interrupted sleep John let out a deep sigh and focused back on the road ahead the car was driving deeper into the forest with the trees growing taller and the sky growing darker Alex felt a sense of unease but he couldn't quite Place why his dad's silence was beginning to make him worried he remembered the argument they had earlier and now with the continuous almost their signs he felt as if they might never reach the cabin Alex looked out the window trying to shake the feeling of worry but the deeper they drove into the forest the more he felt like they were being watched he drifted back to sleep with the rain hitting the roof of the car and the sound of the windshield wipers lulling him to sleep when he next opened his eyes he wasn't sure how much time had passed but he was still in the car and his dad was still driving still silent they continued driving into the night and Alex couldn't shake the feeling that something wasn't right as Alex drifted In and Out Of Consciousness during the long car ride his mind couldn't help but wander to the turmoil between his parents they had been arguing more frequently lately and he couldn't help but feel like it was his fault he wondered if they would ever be happy together or if he was the reason they wanted to get divorced the thought of it brought tears to his eyes and he couldn't help but wish they could all be a happy family again as the storm raged on around them Alex felt the weight of the situation pressed down on him the trip that was supposed to be a well-deserved vacation seemed to be lasting forever his mind raced with thoughts of what could happen if his parents split up how would it affect him where would he live would he ever see them both again he felt overwhelmed and alone but he tried to push those feelings aside reminding himself that they were all in this together John and Sarah were also feeling the strain but they tried to hide it from Alex they glanced at each other occasionally trying to communicate without words they could see the pain in each other's eyes and it broke their hearts but they didn't know how to fix it as the car drove through the Dark Forest Alex finally spoke up Mom Dad I just wanted to say that I love you both so much he said his voice barely above a whisper no matter what happens I'll always love you both John and Sarah looked at Alex their eyes welling up with tears they both smiled at him and then their gazes met the smile faded from their faces as they were reminded of the difficulties they were facing they were both struggling with their own emotions and they didn't know how to reach out to each other I love you too buddy John said his voice choking with emotion will always be a family no matter what Sarah nodded trying to keep her own emotions in check I love you both she said Softly Alex closed his eyes and drifted back to sleep comforted by his parents words but John and Sarah were left to their own thoughts feeling sad and lost as they drove through the Dark Forest they both wanted to be happy together but they didn't know how to fix what was broken between them John drove in silence lost in his own thoughts as the rain continued to pour down outside the car he couldn't shake off the thoughts that had been plaguing him lately thoughts about his work and the immense stress he was under he had been feeling overwhelmed and hopeless thinking about ending his life but the thought of leaving his family behind was too much to bear at work he was constantly being harassed by his boss who would make inappropriate passes at Sarah in front of him but John couldn't do anything about it this along with the mounting stress from work was too much for him to handle and sometimes it made him physically sick as he looked over at Sarah he couldn't help but confess how much he loved and needed her he wanted their relationship to work for the family and he didn't know how to make that happen he wanted to be a good husband and father but he felt like he was failing Sarah I need you to know how much I love and need you I want that relationship to work for the family I don't know how to make that happen but I want to try John's voice was filled with emotion and he couldn't hold back the tears that were forming in his eyes Sarah looked at him her heart aching for him she took his hand and held it tight John I love you too we'll figure this out together we're a team and we'll make it work they shared a tender moment their love for each other and their families shining through in that moment the rain outside the car and the stress of the road trip seemed to fade away as they sat together lost in each other's embrace suddenly John carefully brought the car to a stop his eyes fixed on a large tree blocking the road ahead the family stepped out into the rain their shoes sinking into the mud as they approached the tree what do you think happened Alex asked his voice filled with concern the storm must have knocked it down he speculated looking up at the dark sky overhead but as they gazed at the tree they all felt a strange unease the tree looked as if it had been placed there deliberately not simply fallen over in the storm they looked at each other silently communicating their Mutual uncertainty before shrugging and getting to work moving the tree with all of them working together the tree was soon moved to the side of the road and they piled back into the car eager to continue their Journey to the cabin but Sarah couldn't shake the feeling that something was watching her and she thought she saw a shadowy figure flit across the edge of her vision she brushed it off telling herself it was just her imagination but the fear lingered in the back of her mind as they continued on the Storm raged on outside and the family was more determined than ever to reach their destination they pushed on fighting against the rain and wind and as they drove Sarah couldn't help but think of the strange tree and the shadowy figure she thought she saw the thought was enough to make her shiver and she couldn't wait to reach the safety of the cabin and put the frightening experience behind her as the family continues driving through the storm Sarah's thoughts turned Inward and she became lost in thought guilt consumed her as she reflected on her actions as a wife to John despite being a successful jewelry maker she had made countless mistakes in her marriage the most devastating of which was cheating on Jon with his boss the weight of her infidelity weighed heavily on her every day and she often resorted to drinking to numb the pain as she gazed out the window lost in thought she felt a tap on her shoulder she turned to see John looking at her with a warm and loving gaze I love you he said Softly Sarah's heart felt like it had skipped a beat I love you too she replied her voice trembling with emotion in that moment Sarah couldn't help but feel grateful for John's unwavering love and forgiveness she made a silent promise to herself to be a better wife and to make amends for her past mistakes however the piece of the moment was quickly shattered as the family spotted another almost there sign on the side of the road this time they decided to get out and check it out they approached the sign cautiously feeling a sense of unease the Storm still raged on around them the wind howling through the trees and the rain pelting down relentlessly as they approached the sign they noticed that it was old and weathered looking as though it hadn't been touched in decades despite its state of disrepair it gave the family A glimmer of hope that they were indeed getting closer to their destination they returned to the car eager to reach the cabin and start their much needed vacation

Chapter 4

The family continued driving through the stormy Forest the seemingly never-ending Road was making them feel as if they were lost in a maze suddenly deers began appearing more and more next to the road until the family could no longer drive any further Alex was scared and he turned to his dad asking what they should do John tried to reassure him telling him to stay calm and that he would handle the situation John stepped out of the car and looked at the dares but they were all staring back at him in a moment of frustration he started yelling at them but to no avail in a last-ditch effort John picked up a nearby stick and swung it at the deers which finally made them move away however as John tried to get back into the car several of the deers ran towards him and knocked him down before he could make it inside Sarah and Alex were screaming in Terror as they watched the deer severely injure Jon managed to crawl back into the car bleeding profusely Sarah quickly tried to tend to his wounds but she was in a State of Shock and didn't know what to do the family was stuck in the middle of the forest with no help in sight and John's injuries were getting worse by the minute it was a terrifying and hopeless moment for them and they couldn't help but wonder if they would ever make it out of the forest alive Sarah frantically tries to start the car to get away from the deer but it won't start she tries again and again but nothing happens John is lying in the back seat badly injured and barely conscious Alex is crying and asking if his dad is going to be okay Sarah tells Alex to be brave and that she's going to find help she gets out of the car and starts running through the forest not knowing where she's going but just hoping that she can find someone who can help them the rain is coming down hotter than ever and she's getting more and more scared but she keeps running not giving up as Sarah wandered deeper into the forest she felt herself becoming increasingly lost she tried to retrace her steps but the dense foliage made it difficult to see where she was going her heart was racing with fear and she felt like she was being watched suddenly she tripped on a tree branch and fell to the ground hitting her head on a rock as she lay there slowly losing Consciousness her eyes caught a glimpse of the shadowy figure she had seen earlier she was terrified and struggled to remain conscious in a last-ditch effort to protect her family she mustered all her strength and called out to the shadow begging it to stay away from her loved ones meanwhile back at the car Alex was in a state of panic his father was losing too much blood and the deers were closing in staring at Alex with their unblinking eyes he was overwhelmed with fear and tears began to stream down his face as he cried uncontrollably his father was muttering nonsense and Alex felt completely helpless as he watched him slip into unconsciousness the situation was growing more and more dire and Alex had never felt so alone he closed his eyes and prayed for help hoping that somehow they would all make it out of the forest alive the family was lost so deep in the heart of the forest the darkness was closing in on them from all sides the wind howled through the trees shaking the branches and making them creak ominously the rain beat down upon the car a constant pounding reminder of their situation the deer once so innocent and beautiful now watch them with haunting on blinking eyes as if they were waiting for the family to make a wrong move the family was caught in a storm a Maelstrom of wind and rain that seemed to have no end the family had started out as a happy unit seeking Solace from their troubled lives in a much needed vacation they were a broken family each member struggling with their own demons but they were determined to make this trip work John and Sarah had been married for many years and while they still loved each other the stresses of Life had taken their toll on their relationship Sarah had become distant and often turned to alcohol for Comfort while John worked long hours to provide for his family Alex their son was struggling with his own problems Feeling overshadowed by his parents problems and searching for his place in the world but now all of that seems so far away they were lost deep in a forest that seemed to go on forever the heavy rain and wind made it difficult to see and the Darkness was closing in on them threatening to swallow them whole the deer once so peaceful and Serene now seemed to be closing in on them as well as if they were waiting for an opportunity to attack and Sarah who had wandered away from the car tripped and fell hitting her head on a rock and losing Consciousness was nowhere to be found

Chapter 5

As Alex sat in the car he felt the weight of the situation bearing down on him he watched as his father John lay on the floor of the car bleeding profusely from the deer attack the rain continued to beat against the car and the wind howled reminding Alex of how lost they truly were his mother Sarah was nowhere to be found and Alex was beginning to lose hope that they would ever find her he had never felt so scared and helpless in his life John's breathing was shallow and labored and Alex could see that he was losing consciousness he tried to wake him up but John was unresponsive Alex was filled with a sense of dread as he realized that his father was badly injured and that he was all alone he could hear the deer moving closer to the car their Hooves crunching on the wet ground Alex was afraid that they would attack him too he reached over and grabbed his father's hand squeezing it tightly he closed his eyes and began to pray for help for a miracle for anything that would bring them out of this terrible situation as he prayed he felt a sense of Peace settle over him and he realized that he was not alone they had each other and they would find a way out of the forest together just then Alex heard a voice calling out to him it was Sarah and she was alive she stumbled back to the car her head bleeding in her body bruised but she was alive Alex felt a surge of relief as he helped her into the car and they all huddled together seeking comfort and warmth from each other's embrace they sat there for what felt like ours until the rain finally stopped and the sun began to peek through the clouds they knew that they needed to find help but they were all too injured to move Sarah suggested that Alex go for help and Jon agreed but Alex was afraid to leave them in the end Sarah convinced him that it was the only way to save them and Alex reluctantly agreed Alex stepped out of the car and took a deep breath Looking Down The Long Gravel Road stretching out before him he knew he had to find help but the thought of leaving his injured parents behind made his heartache he thought back to the days leading up to this moment when his family was still whole and happy they had won a paid time off from John's work and decided to use it for a vacation in the woods Alex remembered how excited they all were but now everything had changed as Alex trudged down the gravel road he couldn't help but cast a glance over his shoulder towards the car where his parents were waiting despite the dire circumstances he couldn't help but feel a small glimmer of hope seeing his parents holding each other they had always been a happy family but recent years had taken their toll on their relationship causing tension and distance between them but now as they clung to each other it was as if they were the only two people in the world lost in their own comfort and love Alex had always known that his parents loved each other deeply but seeing them like this filled him with a sense of peace and hope that things could get better for them he was grateful for this small moment of happiness in an otherwise terrible situation as he continued down the road Alex took comfort in the thought that at least his parents had each other even if they were lost in the middle of nowhere he knew that finding help was crucial but taking one last look at his parents he felt a weight lifted from his shoulders for a moment everything felt a little bit better and with that Alex turned back to the road ahead determined to do everything in his power to find help for his family as Alex stepped away from the car and began his long walk down the gravel road his parents were left alone with their thoughts John and Sarah were in a State of Shock unable to process the fact that their son had just ventured out into the unknown in search of help but amidst all the chaos they found solace in each other's arms they sat there in silence holding each other tight and savoring the moment of comfort Sarah buried her head in John's chest feeling the steady beat of his heart and he ran his fingers through her hair trying to calm her for the first time in a long time John and Sarah felt like a family again all the worries and Troubles of their everyday lives seemed so far away they had each other and in that moment that was all that mattered as they sat there they couldn't help but think of Alex and how he was faring on his search for help they hoped and prayed that he was okay that he was safe and that he would soon come back to them with help do you think he'll be okay Sarah asked breaking the silence of course he will John said trying to sound reassuring Alex is strong he's smart and he's a fighter he'll find help and he'll be back before we know it Sarah nodded and the two of them continued to hold each other both lost in their thoughts but comforted by the fact that they had each other as Alex continued his search for help he stumbled upon a herd of deer blocking the road ahead the deer looked half dead their eyes dull and glassy and their once graceful bodies now thin and gaunt Alex's heart raced as he realized that they were trapped with no way to get around the animals panicking he turned and ran back to the car where his parents were waiting he told them about the herd of deer blocking their path and that they had no choice but to leave the car and continue their Journey on foot Sarah and John nodded their expressions tense and they decided to wait out the night until morning so they could take a moment to rest from the injuries once the morning came they gathered what supplies they could carry and set out into the forest once again this time with a newfound sense of urgency the herd of deer continued to block their path their lifeless eyes seeming to follow the family as they walked by as they continued their Journey the family couldn't help but feel like they were being watched the deer were no longer just blocking their path they were a constant presence reminding the family of their vulnerability and the danger that surrounded them despite the overwhelming odds against them the family refused to give up hope they were determined to survive and they knew that they had to stay together to do so with each step they grew more determined more Resolute in their mission to find help and escape the endless Forest as the sun began to set casting Long Shadows across the forest floor the family pressed on despite their fatigue and the growing fear they refused to stop refused to give in to the terror that threatened to consume them as they traveled through the forest the thick underbrush made it difficult to move forward the family had to push aside branches and brambles as they went their Pace slow and deliberate the only sounds were the crunching of leaves and twigs underfoot and the occasional snap of a branch

Alex was on high alert his heart pounding in his chest the thought of getting lost in this never-ending forest was a constant fear but he pushed it aside he had to be strong for his parents who were relying on him to lead the way despite the thick foliage the family continued on determined to find help they had been driving for hours before they got lost and they were all exhausted but they didn't let that stop them they were a family and they would make it through this together as they walked the forest started to change the trees grew taller their branches stretching up towards the sky like fingers reaching for the Sun the underbrush grew thicker making it even more difficult to move forward but the family pushed on their feet pounding the soft Earth as they went with each step the family grew more and more tired but they refused to give up they were going to find help no matter what it took and so with a fierce determination they continued on their eyes fixed on the path ahead as they walked deeper and deeper into the endless Forest

Chapter 6

While the family continued on they started to feel a sense of unease the forest felt endless and they couldn't find a way out they started to panic as they realized that they were lost and couldn't find their way back to the car John tried to keep calm but he too was starting to feel overwhelmed Sarah clung to him in fear Alex was scared too but he tried to hide it for the sake of his parents as the sun disappeared the family realized that they would have to spend the night in the forest they set up camp huddled together for warmth and comfort they tried to remain positive but the fear of being lost in the endless forest was starting to take its toll on them that night as they huddled together they could hear strange noises coming from the darkness they were scared but they tried to stay calm telling each other that it was just the sounds of the forest but as the night went on the noises grew louder and the family realized that something was definitely not right they clutched each other tightly unsure of what the future held the next morning the family tried to find a way out of the forest they walked for hours but no matter which way they turned they always ended up back at their campsite it was as if they were stuck in an endless loop unable to escape the forest the days kept getting longer and the family started to run low on supplies they were becoming weak and desperate their hope of ever finding a way out fading as they hiked they started to notice strange occurrences they would find their own Footprints leading them in a circle or they would come across objects that they had left behind but in different locations it was as if the forest was playing tricks on them leading them in a never-ending maze the family was starting to lose their grip on reality John became distant and paranoid while Sarah started to spiral into depression Alex was the only one who remained somewhat sane but he too was starting to feel the effects of the endless loop they were trapped unable to escape the grasp of the mysterious Forest and as each day passed they were pulled deeper into its hold unsure if they would ever find their way out the family continued their Journey Through the endless Forest But as time passed they started to deteriorate John became distant and paranoid constantly looking over his shoulder and jumping at any small noise Sarah's depression deepened and she stopped talking altogether spending most of her time lying in the tent and humming tunes that she used to sing to Alex when he was a baby Alex tried to keep his parents spirits up but it was becoming increasingly difficult he noticed that his own thoughts and memories were starting to become muddled as if the forest was trying to take over his mind the one slush forest was becoming darker and more Sinister with each passing day the trees were closer together and the undergrowth was thicker it was as if the forest was closing in on them trying to swallow them the family was running low on food and water and they were starting to see things that couldn't possibly be real John claimed to see Shadows moving in the trees and Sarah whispered about hearing whispers in the Wind Alex was starting to fear that they would never escape the forest and that they would be trapped there forever their situation was becoming more and more dire with each passing day and they were starting to lose hope they had entered the forest as a happy family but now they were on the brink of Destruction their love and bond tested by the forest the family's Spirits hit rock bottom as they realized that they had been walking in circles for days John started to become manic convinced that they were being followed by something in the forest and started yelling into the forest Sarah withdrew further into herself barely speaking or eating Alex tried to keep a positive attitude but he was becoming exhausted both physically and mentally one night as they huddled around their campfire John snapped he screamed at Sarah blaming her for getting them lost in the forest in the first place Sarah fought back revealing that she had cheated on Jon with his boss and that she was the reason they were on this hike to begin with John was Furious and the two of them got into a physical altercation Alex was horrified by what he was seeing he had never seen his parents fight like this before there was supposed to be a happy family and now they were tearing each other apart after the fight the family was even more broken John and Sarah barely spoke to each other and Alex felt like he was the only thing holding them together he didn't know what to do or how to fix things all he knew was that they needed to get out of the forest and fast with a renewed sense of hope the family continued their search for a way out of the forest Alex took the lead using his knowledge of navigation to guide them John followed his hand tightly gripping a knife that he had fashioned from a branch ready to protect his family if necessary Sarah trailed behind her spirits lifted by the thought of finally finding their way home as they walked

Alex couldn't help but think about the fight between his parents he was determined to bring them back together but he wasn't sure how despite the tense atmosphere he was grateful for the love and support they still showed each other even in the face of adversity suddenly Alex spotted something in the distance it was a cabin and it looked all too familiar with a burst of energy he ran towards it with his parents following close behind as they reached the cabin they realized it was their own the one they had been searching for this entire time overwhelmed with relief the family embraced each other tears of joy streaming down their faces they had finally found their way to the cabin the place where they would feel safe and loved the journey through the endless Forest felt like it was finally over and they could rest and begin to heal from the trials they had faced

Chapter 7

After what felt like aneternity the family finally stumbledupon the entrance to the cabin they hadrented for their vacationit had been days since they were lastable to take a shower or even change outof their damp and dirty clothesas soon as they step through the frontdoor they each let out a sigh of reliefJohn was the first to break the silencelet's get cleaned up and eat somethingI'm starvingthe rest of the family nodded inagreement and quickly went to workSarah started a fire in the fireplace towarm up the cabin while Alex went togather firewood once they were allsettled they each took turns showeringfinally feeling clean for the first timein what felt like agesSarah started cooking up a simple mealof pasta and sauce grateful for thesmall Comforts of homeas they ate they talked and laughedrelishing in their Newfound safety andcomfortas the night wore on they each retiredto their own rooms exhausted from thetrials they had facedSarah who was the last one awake stoodat the kitchen sink peering out thewindow while she prepared a late nightsnack she couldn't shake the feelingthat something was watching hershe brushed it off as exhaustion fromtheir harrowing journey through theforest but as she continued to gaze outinto the darkness she noticed a figurestanding in the distance partiallyobscured by the treesat first Sarah thought it was just atrick of the light but as she lookedcloser she realized it was a personshe rubbed her eyes trying to clear hervision but the figure was still thereSarah's heart started pounding in herchest and she felt a pain in her head asif it was being squeezed a sharp pain inher nose made her wince and she lookeddown to see a trail of blood tricklingfrom one nostril panicking Sarah turnedfrom the window and stumbled to the doorcalling out for Johnshe felt dizzy and her vision wasstarting to blurhas she opened the door John was theregun in hand ready to protect his familywhat's wrong he asked his voice sharpand concerned Sarah told him about thefigures she saw outside and how her headwas hurtingJohn didn't hesitatehe ran outside shouting into the nightwarning the figure to stay away from hisfamilyas John stood guard outside the cabinSarah collapsed onto the couch her headpounding with painshe closed her eyes hoping that when sheopened them again everything would bealrightbut she couldn't shake the feeling thatthey were being watched and thatsomething sinister was lurking in theshadows of the forestthe sound of shouting and gunfireoutside jolted Alex out of his deepsleephe quickly sat up in his bed lookingaround confused and disoriented hecouldn't believe that this was happeningagain he had thought they were safe nowthat they had finally made it to thecabin but apparently he was wronghe raced to the door his heart poundingin his chest and tried to open it to hishorror the door wouldn't budgehe was trappedhe started to panic Breathing heavilyand desperately tried to find a way outhe tried to use his body weight to pushit open but it wouldn't movehe searched for anything he could use tobreak the door down grabbing his lampand Swinging it at the handle but itonly bounced off with a loud thud Alexfrantically started to pound his fistsagainst the door desperate to get outand help his parentshis knuckles began to ache and he couldfeel the bones straining against hisskin as he put more and more Force intoeach blowdespite his increasing pain he refusedto stop the fear for his family fueledhis determination and he continued tobeat against the door with all his mightas his knuckles started to bleed he feltone of his bones snapthe pain was excruciating but still hedidn't stophe howled in frustration and anger as hethrew his shoulder against the doorhoping to break it downhe could hear his dad shouting andshooting outside and he knew that he hadto get to himtears streamed down Alex's face as hecontinued to batter the doorhe didn't know how long he had beenpounding on it but it felt like aneternityhis breasts were coming in short gaspsand his whole body was drenched in sweathe was starting to feel like he waslosing the battle but still he refusedto give upfinally with one final burst of energythe door gave way and Alex stumbled outinto the hallwayhe could hear the shouting and shootingfrom outside getting louder and he racedtowards the source of the noise as fastas his broken hand would allowdespite the pain he pushed on until hearrived in the living roomas he looked around the room forsomething anything to help his dadoutside he saw his mother on the couchseizing a dark ominous Shadow wasstanding over her and Alex was Frozenwith fearhe had never seen anything like itbeforebut he knew he needed to help his motheras he ran past his mother he stopped fora moment to tell her not to worryhe promised her that he would get Dadand everything would be okay but as hemade his way outside he couldn't shakethe feeling of dread that was creepingover himwhen he reached his dad they could seefrom outside that Sarah was having aseizure on the couch and there was ashadow figure standing over her Alex'sheart was pounding in his chest as heran back inside with his dadbut when they got back his mom and thefigure were both gone and the door hadslammed shutAlex was filled with a mixture of fearand confusion as he tried to make senseof what was happening just as everythingstopped John caught a glimpse of theshadowy figure running through the woodswith Sarah's lifeless body and heimmediately takes aim at the shadowyfigure his heart was pounding in hischesthe knew this could be the moment thatdecided whether his family would surviveor nothe took a deep breath steadied his handand pulled the trigger the sound of thegun echoed throughout the forest and inan instant everything changedJohn felt a sharp pain in his mouth andhe realized that the bullet hadricocheted off a tree and hit him hestumbled back trying to gasp for air butit was no usethe blood was gushing from his mouthfilling his lungs and choking him todeathJohn stumbled backwards choking andcoughing as blood spewed from his mouthAlex was horrified and he tried to catchhis dad before he hit the groundhe cradled Jon in his arms tearsstreaming down his face as he watchedhis father slowly diethe last thing John did was look up atAlex with a pained expression before hetook his final breath Alex sat there inshock unable to process what had justhappenedhe had lost his mother to a mysteriousfigure and now his father was gone toohe felt alone and helpless but he knewthat he needed to stay strong for hisfamilyhe gently placed his father's body onthe ground and then he went back outsideto begin searching for his mother

Chapter 8

Alex was in a panic his mother Sarah had disappeared and his father John lay dead on the floor blood pooling around him he had never felt so helpless and alone in his life he stumbled through the cabin his mind racing as he tried to figure out what to do next he knew he had to find his mother but he was afraid to go out into the woods alone he needed a weapon something to protect himself with he made his way to the kitchen hoping to find a knife or a heavy object that he could use as a weapon he Inked open the drawers and cupboards tossing utensils and plates aside in his search he found a cast iron skillet and hefted it in his hand testing its weight it would have to do next he moved to the living room where his father's hunting rifles were stored he had never fired a gun before but he knew his father had taught him how he selected the heaviest rifle one that his father had used on many hunting trips and checked to see if it was loaded it was and Alex felt a small sense of relief he slung the rifle over his shoulder and took the skillet in his other hand he stood in the doorway of the cabin peering out into the darkness of the forest he could see the Shadows of the trees and the faint glow of the Moon he took a deep breath and stepped outside his heart pounding in his chest he made his way down the path his eyes scanning the trees for any sign of his mother or the shadowy figure as he walked he called out to his mother his voice shaking there was no answer he walked for what felt like ours his mind racing as he tried to think of where she could have gone the woods were dense and treacherous and he was afraid of getting lost he tried to remain calm to keep his wits about him but it was difficult he had never felt so alone and scared in his life He Walked on his mind and heart filled with fear and hope hoping that he would find his mother and bring her back to safety Alex's frustration grew with every step he took he had been walking for hours searching for his missing mother and every tree and rock seemed to blend together into a never-ending maze he thought he was making progress but now he wasn't so sure as he walked he noticed that the same Twisted oak tree was coming into view for the third time that was when it hit him he was lost the forest was playing tricks on his mind and leading him in circles he stopped in his tracks feeling a wave of anger wash over him he looked up at the sky as if searching for an answer and let out a scream stop playing games with me he yelled into the forest just leave us alone tears streamed down his face as he continued to shout his voice-growing horse he felt like he was at the end of his rope completely helpless in this endless Forest he didn't know how to find his mother or even if she was still alive the fear and uncertainty were too much for him to bear but despite all of his anger and frustration he refused to give up he was determined to find his mother no matter what he took a deep breath trying to calm himself and wiped away his tears Alex continued his journey through the dense forest his heart racing with both fear and determination suddenly he spotted a herd of deer in the distance he slowed down trying to be as quiet as possible as he snuck past them but as soon as he was within a few feet of the herd they suddenly became aware of his presence their heads shot up their eyes locking onto Alex's for a moment they simply stared at each other both Alex and the deer Frozen in place then without warning the deer suddenly charged towards Alex he tried to dodge out of the way but one of the deer caught him with a strong Buck sending him tumbling to the ground the herd descended upon Him their Hooves pounding against his flesh Alex tried to get back up but the Relentless assault from the deer kept knocking him back down he lay there his body battered and bloodied As the deer continued their attack he could feel his Consciousness slipping away and for a moment he feared that this would be the end for him but then an idea popped into his head he lays still pretending to be dead hoping that the deer would eventually lose interest and leave him alone the ruse seemed to work and after a few long moments the deer became neutral leaving him alone as Alex lay on the forest floor pretending to be dead he could feel the herd of deer lingering around him despite the danger he was in he couldn't open his eyes not even a crack he was completely still trying to slow his breathing and listening intently to the sounds around him the deer were sniffing him snorting and shuffling around him but they didn't leave they stayed there for hours waiting As Time passed Alex faded in and out of consciousness he thought about his family and the horrible turn of events that had led him to this moment he thought about his father John and How brave he was to face the shadow figure and try to protect the family he thought about his mother Sarah who was now lost and alone in the forest and he thought about himself how he was barely holding on lying on the forest floor surrounded by a herd of dangerous deer despite the physical pain and fear that consumed him Alex couldn't help but feel grateful for the moments of clarity he had in between consciousness these moments allowed him to reflect on his life and his family he realized how much he loved and needed them and how much he wanted to see them again but as he lay there surrounded by the deer it seemed like that might never happen as the hours passed Alex's thoughts became cloudier his hold on reality slipping away he couldn't tell if he was awake or asleep alive or dead but even in his state of confusion he couldn't help but wonder if this was the end for him if he would ever see his family again as Alex lays on the forest floor pretending to be dead he drifts in and out of consciousness in one of his Lucid moments he begins to dream the dream at first is a happy one where his family is together laughing and enjoying each other's company but as the dream progresses the tone takes a dark turn the Sun is setting and the family is gathered around the fire pit roasting marshmallows and telling stories suddenly the sound of hooves can be heard in the distance and a herd of deer emerges from the forest the family is initially excited to see the Beautiful Creatures but their excitement turns to fear As the deer start to Circle them in the dream Alex is paralyzed with fear he tries to warn his family but he can't seem to make a sound the herd of deer suddenly attack and Alex watches in horror as they Massacre his family in a gruesome scene the family is unable to defend themselves and the deer use their sharp Hooves and antlers to tear them apart Alex wakes up in a cold sweat the vivid dreams still fresh in his mind he realizes that he's been lying on the ground for hours and the deer are still surrounding him waiting the dream has left him feeling vulnerable scared and alone he's never felt so helpless and the thought of losing his family is tearing him apart as the hours passed Alex started to feel the deer's presence diminish he still lay there pretending to be dead waiting for them to leave completely suddenly he heard the rustling of leaves and twigs snapping under Hooves moving further away from him he was finally alone but he was badly hurt with cuts bruises and scrapes all over his body he felt weak but he knew he had to find his mom he had to keep searching for her to add to the weight of the situation Vivid memories of his father dying earlier in the night continued to haunt him he took a deep breath and tried to get up but he felt an intense pain in his ribs and he fell back to the ground he laid there for a few more minutes trying to gather his strength and then he tried again this time he managed to get up but he felt dizzy and unsteady he leaned against the tree for support and took a moment to catch his breath finally he started walking stumbling at times but still determined to keep going he walked for what felt like ours searching for any sign of his mom shouting her name and calling for her he felt like he was losing hope but he couldn't give up he had to keep going he had to find her

Chapter 9

Sarah found herself laying on the ground of a dark damp cave paralyzed and unable to move she was completely in the dark and could see nothing all she could do was listen and pray that whatever was happening to her would end soon suddenly she heard a faint rustling noise and a strong pungent odor wafted towards her it was then that she realized that something or someone was approaching her the shadowy figure came closer and closer its presence growing stronger with each step Sarah could feel its hot breath on her hair and she realized that it was sniffing her the figure was so close to her now that she could feel its weight on the ground beside her she tried to scream but no sound escaped her mouth suddenly the figure started to climb on the walls of the cave its movements accompanied by the most horrific sounds Sarah had ever heard the creature was making its way around the cave scraping its nails against the rough walls and growling in a low guttural voice Sarah was frozen in Terror unable to move as the creature continued its approach all the while Sarah could only think of Jon she hoped that he was okay she lay there in the dark unable to move as the shadowy figure continued to Circle her its hot breath on her neck and its frightening sounds echoing off the walls of the cave As Time passed Sarah could feel herself starting to fade in and out despite her fear she clung to the hope that Jon was still out there somewhere fighting to protect her and their family hours go by while Sarah lays in the dark cold cave body paralyzed and unable to move suddenly she heard a feigned voice calling out her name and her heart left with hope it was Alex her son and he was searching for her she tried with all her might to scream out to him to tell him to run the other way but her voice was gone lost in the Darkness tears streamed down her face as she realized she was helpless unable to warn or protect him suddenly she heard the footsteps of the shadow figure that had been haunting her family getting closer and closer she knew it was going after Alex and the thought of him being in Danger made her heart race with fear she closed her eyes tightly tears streaming down her face as she listened to the sound of the shadow figure getting closer and closer to her son she was powerless to stop it unable to save him from the darkness that had engulfed their family she lay there crying hysterically as the footsteps grew distant and finally faded away Into the Night the fear of the unknown and the fear of what could have happened to Alex consumed her mind as she lay there in the dark cold cave she hoped with all her heart that he was safe but she knew deep down that the shadow figure was hunting him and she was powerless to do anything about it as Alex continues to call out for his mother his voice grows louder and more desperate he can hear her faint cries in the distance but they are muffled and garbled Alex starts to run towards the sound of her voice but with each step he realizes how lost he truly is the dense trees and underbrush make it difficult to see more than a few feet in front of him and he feels as though the forest is closing in on him despite the fear gnawing at his gut Alex presses on determined to find his mother and bring her to safety he calls up for her again and this time he hears a faint response he quickens his Pace dodging around trees and leaping over Fallen logs just as he thinks he's getting close he hears a blood curdling growl from behind him he spins around but all he sees is Darkness he tries to run in the opposite direction but the growling grows louder and he can hear the sound of heavy footsteps pounding the ground Alex knows that the shadow figure is closing in on him and he starts to panic he stumbles nearly falling and cries out for his mother in his desperation he raises his rifle and blindly fires into the darkness the sound of the shot Echoes through the forest but all that greets Alex's silence trembling he calls out for his mother once more but there is no response the shadow figure has gone after her leaving Alex alone in the woods he falls to his knees tears streaming down his face and lets out a heart-wrenching scream the forest is silent except for the sound of Alex's sobs as he realizes that he may never see his mother or father again as Alex continued to call out for his mother the shadow figure slowly made its way back into the cave Sarah could hear its painful whimpers as if it had been hurt by The Gunshot Alex had fired earlier suddenly it lunged forward and scraped its sharp claws across Sarah's leg causing her to scream out in pain but just as quickly as it had appeared the shadowy figure disappeared into the Shadows leaving Sarah injured and alone in the Darkness terrified and in pain Sarah could hear Alex's footsteps growing closer he cautiously made his way into the cave calling out for her when he finally reached her he saw that she was wounded and bleeding he quickly went to her side trying to assess the damage and provide comfort Mom are you okay he asked his voice shaking with fear and concern could only nod tears streaming down her face as she tried to hold back her Subs Alex gently lifted her into his arms cradling her close as he made his way back out of the cave and into the daylight with his mother injured and the shadow figure still lurking nearby Alex knew that he had to keep them both safe and find a way to get them out of the woods has Alex and his mother made their way back through the woods they were on high alert for any danger that may come their way the Journey Back to the cabin was slow and grueling as Sarah was injured and needed help from Alex to walk despite their exhaustion they kept moving forward determined to make it back to safety along the way they encountered a herd of deer but this time the deer were not aggressive they simply stared at Alex and Sarah for a moment before returning to their grazing Alex and Sarah took this as a good sign believing that the worst of their Journey was behind them as they finally made it back to the cabin Sarah's heart sank as she saw John's lifeless body lying on the ground she let out a blood curdling scream and fell to her knees tears streaming down her face why did this have to happen she cried cursing the forest and everything in it Alex tried his best to comfort his mother but he was also grappling with his own grief and fear he was grateful to be back at the cabin but he was also scared of what may come next he held Sarah close trying to provide her with comfort and security but he couldn't shake the feeling that their Journey was far from over.as they both grieved for Jon and tried to make sense of what had happened Alex and Sarah made a vow to each other to stay together and support one another no matter what they were stronger together than apart and they were thankful to be alive later on Alex and his mother finally mustered up the courage to make their way back to the car they had been preparing for this moment since they arrived back at the cabin Gathering supplies and going over their plan the sun was beginning to rise and the woods looked peaceful unlike the last time they saw it Alex and his mother said one last goodbye to John's lifeless body before they departed to the car despite the warmth they couldn't shake the feeling of unease as they made their way back through the trees the sound of their footsteps seemed to be echoing louder and louder as if the forest was trying to remind them of what happened before as they approached the car they expected the worst but to their surprise the car was there waiting for them as if it was untouched the keys were still in the ignition and the engine started with alohum Alex and Sarah were finally able to escape the woods that haunted them for what felt like an eternity as they drove out of the woods they saw the herd of deer that had been following them for days this time the deer didn't chase them or try to attack them they simply looked at the car as it passed as if watching them leave Alex just wanted to forget everything that had happened he didn't want to think about the deer anymore he just wanted to be back home in Fenton Missouri where he felt safe finally after what felt like an endless Drive they arrived back in their hometown the site of their house was a welcome relief and they both started crying with joy they had made it back home back to where they felt safe and back to their old lives

Chapter 10

It had been a month since the traumatic events that took place in the woods Alex and his mother Sarah were trying their best to cope with their lives now but it was not an easy task the memories of what had happened were fresh in their minds haunting them day and night every time they closed their eyes they were transported back to that dark and Eerie Place filled with fear and horror they had both suffered physical and emotional wounds that would take a long time to heal Sarah's legs still ached from the deep scratch that the shadow figure had inflicted upon her before it disappeared into the darkness Alex was plagued by guilt feeling as though he could have done more to protect his family he struggled with Nightmares of the deer attack and the memory of his dad dying in his arms was always in the back of his mind the two of them had tried to go back to their normal routines but it was just a facade they had lost John and the memory of his death was a constant source of pain Sarah had quit her job unable to focus on anything besides the grief that consumed her Alex had dropped out of school and was spending most of his days holed up in his room lost in his own thoughts their life had been forever changed by what had happened in the woods and they were still trying to come to terms with their new reality they sought comfort in each other but it was a constant struggle to find even a glimmer of hope in their shattered lives they were both haunted by the memories of what had happened and it seemed as though they would never truly escape the terror that had taken hold of their lives As Time passed Alex and his mother struggled to come to terms with the traumatic events they had experienced in the forest they both felt a strong need to find meaning in what had happened in order to make sense of it all they were haunted by the loss of John and were consumed by the need to understand why they had been targeted Sarah and Alex started doing extensive research into the forest searching for any information they could find about its history Legends and mysterious occurrences they scoured through old books maps and articles trying to piece together the puzzle of what had happened to them they talked to anyone who had any knowledge of the forest they also talked to locals who had lived in the area for their entire lives hoping to gain some insight into the strange and frightening World they had found themselves in through their research they discovered that the forest was once home to a powerful Native American tribe who had lived there for Generations they learned about the tribe's Legends and spiritual beliefs and how they believed that the forest was protected by powerful spirits who would only reveal themselves to those who were pure of heart and had the courage to face their fears Alex and Sarah also learned about the numerous reports of strange noises and sights in the forest and how many people had gone missing there over the years as they delved deeper into the mystery they realized that they may never fully understand what had happened to them but they felt a sense of comfort in trying to make sense of it all they were determined to find a way to cope with their loss and to help others who may find themselves in the same situation they knew that it would be a long and difficult Journey but they were both committed to finding peace and healing for themselves and more importantly for John and so the sun was setting on the small town of Fenton Missouri as Alex and Sarah drove down the quiet streets finally back in the comfort of their own home the warm light of the sun cast The Golden Glow over the neighborhood Illuminating the lush green trees and well-manicured lawns as they approached their home they couldn't help but feel a sense of Peace wash over them after all they had been through in the mysterious Forest being back in their familiar surroundings was like a bomb to their souls they pulled into the driveway and stepped out of the car stretching their legs and taking in the sights and sounds of home they looked at each other and smiled both grateful to have made it back safely the wind rustled through the leaves of the trees and the sound of children playing in the distance filled the air the horrors of the past month seemed like a distant memory now and as Alex and Sarah walked hand in hand towards their front door they were filled with hope for a brighter future